For Mai and Cam – J.D.   For Florence – N.S.

PUFFIN BOOKS

Published by the Penguin Group
Penguin Books Ltd, 80 Strand, London WC2R 0RL, England
Penguin Putnam Inc., 375 Hudson Street, New York, New York 10014, USA
Penguin Books Australia Ltd, 250 Camberwell Road, Camberwell, Victoria 3124, Australia
Penguin Books Canada Ltd, 10 Alcorn Avenue, Toronto, Ontario, Canada M4V 3B2
Penguin Books India (P) Ltd, 11 Community Centre, Panchsheel Park, New Delhi – 110 017, India
Penguin Books (NZ) Ltd, Cnr Rosedale and Airborne Roads, Albany, Auckland, New Zealand
Penguin Books (South Africa) (Pty) Ltd, 24 Sturdee Avenue, Rosebank 2196, South Africa

www.penguin.com

Penguin Books Ltd, Registered Offices: 80 Strand, London WC2R 0RL, England

First published 2003
3 5 7 9 10 8 6 4 2

Text copyright © Julia Donaldson, 2003
Illustrations copyright © Nick Sharratt, 2003

The moral right of the author and illustrator has been asserted

Set in Ablib BT

Made and printed in China

British Library Cataloguing in Publication Data
A CIP catalogue record for this book is available from the British Library

ISBN 0-140-56848-4

Conjuror Cow

JULIA DONALDSON **NICK SHARRATT**

PUFFIN BOOKS

Everyone's waiting.
The lights have
gone low.

Abracadabra
and Rat-a-tat-tat!
I can make a
white rabbit...

...come out of this cake!

Abracadabra
and Broccoli Broth!
White rabbit,
you'd better be . . .

Lots of
white rabbits
all taking
a bow!